The Pet Finders Club

4. Snake Alarm!

Illustrated by Jan Lewis

BARRON'S

First edition for the United States, Canada, and the Philippines published by Barron's Educational Series, Inc., 1998.

First published in Great Britain in 1997 by Scholastic Children's Books, Commonwealth House, 1-19 New Oxford Street, London WC1A 1NU, UK
A division of Scholastic Ltd

All inquiries should be addressed to:

Barron's Educational Series, Inc.
250 Wireless Boulevard
Hauppauge, New York 11788
http://www.barronseduc.com

ISBN 0-7641-0573-6
Library of Congress Catalog Card No. 97-38851

Library of Congress Cataloging-in-Publication Data

Krailing, Tessa, 1935-
    The Petsitters Club. 4, Snake alarm! / Tessa Krailing.—1st ed.
        p. cm.
    Summary: Because neither Sam nor her father realizes that a garter snake dropped off for "petsitting" has escaped, they can't understand Aunt Cynthia's alarming shrieks.
    ISBN 0-7641-0573-6
    [1. Garter snakes—Fiction. 2. Snakes—Fiction. 3. Aunts—Fiction. 4. Clubs—Fiction.] I. Title.
PZ7.K85855Sn 1998
[Fic]—dc21   97-38851
                                                              CIP
                                                              AC

Printed in the United States of America
9 8 7 6 5 4 3 2 1

Chapter 1

No Problem

Matthew was playing a video game when the doorbell rang. He ignored it, hoping that somebody else would answer. When nobody did, he groaned and went downstairs.

Greg Tutt stood on the doorstep, clutching a large plastic box with holes in the lid.

"I have an emergency," said Greg, who was in the same class as Matthew at school. "My grandmother is sick, so we have to go and visit her. Could the Petsitters Club take care of Gertie for me while I'm away?"

"No problem," said Matthew, holding out his hand for the box.

But Greg seemed reluctant to part with it. "You will take care of her, won't you?"

"I told you, no problem," said Matthew, who was in a hurry to get back to his video game. "We Petsitters are used to taking care of all kinds of pets. What is Gertie, anyway?"

"A garter snake." Greg lifted the lid to show him.

Matthew peered down at the slender brown snake with three yellow stripes running down its back. Actually he wasn't crazy about snakes. He wasn't afraid of them exactly, he just didn't like the way they wriggled.

"Does she bite?" he asked cautiously.

"No, she's very friendly," Greg assured him.

"What does she eat?"

"Small fish mostly. Or worms. But she won't need to be fed again for at least three days and I think I'll be back by then."

Matthew was relieved. The idea of feeding worms to Gertie made him feel kind of queasy.

Greg closed the lid. "This is only her traveling box. Do you have a terrarium to keep her in?"

"What's a terrarium?" asked Matthew.

"It's like an empty fish tank with gravel on the bottom."

"Oh, my sister Katie has one of those. She's the expert on creepy-crawlies. She'll take good care of Gertie for you."

Reverently Greg handed over the box. "Do I have to pay you something?"

Matthew shook his head. "We do it for the community service project at school. You just have to sign a form so we can get points for it, that's all."

"I'm trying to get points, too," said Greg, still reluctant to leave his pet. "I've been cleaning people's cars and stuff like that."

"Yeah, well . . ." Matthew started to close the front door. "Bye, Greg."

"You will keep Gertie warm, won't you?"

"Of course," Matthew promised and firmly closed the door.

He carried the box upstairs to his room and put it on the dresser. Then he settled down to his video game. Now, where was I when the doorbell rang? he thought. Oh yes, the Demon Raider had just been zapped by the Lord of the Universe.

But it was no use, he couldn't concentrate. His gaze kept straying to the plastic box. This was the first time the Petsitters Club had been asked to take care of a snake. Usually they took care of more ordinary pets like cats and dogs. Petsitting had seemed a great way to earn points for the school's community service project, but now he wasn't so sure. Taking care of a snake was a big responsibility. What if it escaped? He got up to make sure the lid was on firmly, and at that moment his younger sister Katie came into the room.

"There you are!" he said, relieved. "Didn't you hear the doorbell ring?"

"No, I was in the garden, collecting bugs. Who was it?"

"Greg Tutt. He brought his pet for you to take care of while he's away."

"Why me?" asked Katie. "Is it a creepy-crawly?"

"Sort of. Her name's Gertie and she's in that box."

Katie lifted the lid and peered inside. "That's not a creepy-crawly," she said, disappointed. "It's a snake."

"Snakes *are* creepy-crawlies," said Matthew.

"No, they're not. They're slippery-slitherers." She closed the lid. "Creepy-crawlies have legs."

"Anyway," continued Matthew, "I promised you'd take care of her for Greg. I said you'd put her in your tank."

"Well, you shouldn't have," Katie said crossly. "My tank's already full. I'm using it to keep my barnacles in."

"*Barnacles!*" Matthew stared at her. "You mean those crusty things that get stuck to boats?"

Katie nodded. "They're my latest pets."

"But they don't have any legs either, so they can't be creepy-crawlies. They're not even alive."

"Ha!" Katie said triumphantly. "That shows how little you know. Because barnacles *are* alive and they *do* have

legs. You can see them waving in the water." She went to the door.

"Hey, where are you going?" asked Matthew.

"Out shopping with Mom."

"But, but what am I supposed to do with Gertie?"

Katie shrugged. "Take care of her yourself. Or ask Sam to look after her."

"Sam's busy. She has an old aunt staying for the weekend."

"Then I guess you'll have to ask Jo. Bye, Matthew."

The door closed behind her.

Matthew sighed. He turned off the video and picked up the plastic box.

Chapter 2

A Snake Called Gertie

Jovan was working on his stamp collection when the doorbell rang. He ignored it, hoping that somebody else would answer. When nobody did, he groaned and went downstairs.

Matthew stood on the doorstep, clutching a plastic box with holes in the lid.

"We have an emergency," he said. "Greg Tutt's given us his pet to take care of while he's away. Only I'm busy, and so's Katie, so I've brought it over for you to take care of instead." He held out the box.

Jovan looked at it suspiciously. "What is it?"

"A garter snake." He thrust the box into Jovan's hands. "Her name's Gertie."

Jovan swallowed hard. "Did you say a snake?"

"Yes, but she's not very big and she doesn't bite. Greg says she won't need to be fed for at least three days and he'll be back by then. Okay?"

"No, it's not okay. I don't . . ."

"Bye, Jo." Matthew turned and ran down the path before Jovan had a chance to tell him that he didn't like snakes. Suddenly, Matthew was out of sight.

Slowly Jovan closed the front door. He stared down at the box.

Did it really contain a snake? It felt so light, and it looked so harmless.

Cautiously he lifted the lid and looked inside.

Oh, great! It was definitely a snake.

Hastily he put the lid back into place.

Mom came out of the kitchen, carrying a paintbrush, "Sorry I couldn't answer the door, but I was up on the ladder. Who was it?"

"Matthew," said Jovan. "He brought somebody's pet for me to take care of. It's a . . . a snake and she's named Gertie."

"How fascinating," said Mom, who was interested in all kinds of wildlife and never missed a single nature program on TV. "May I look?"

Silently he handed her the box.

She lifted the lid and peered inside. "How beautiful!" she exclaimed. "I love those yellow stripes down its back. Did Matthew tell you what kind it is?"

"I think he said it was a garter snake."

"I've heard of those. They're harmless snakes." She closed the lid and handed back the box. "You should show your father when he comes home. Now I'd better continue with my painting."

She disappeared into the kitchen.

Jovan closed the front door and put the box down carefully on the hall table. Unfortunately he didn't share his mother's enthusiasm for wildlife. The only reason he had been invited to join the Petsitters Club was because his father was a vet. The other members—Sam, Matthew and Katie—thought this meant he must know a lot about animals, but he didn't. He didn't even like them very much, and he certainly didn't like reptiles. He decided to leave the box on the table and try to forget it was there.

"Mom," he said, following her into the kitchen. "Can I help you?"

"Yes, of course. Grab a paintbrush."

When Dad came home he called out, "Sorry I'm late. Had to go and see a man about some pigs."

"Don't worry," Mom called back from the kitchen. "We only just finished painting. Dinner won't be ready for half an hour, I'm afraid."

"How's it going?" Dad stuck his head around the door. "Oh, that looks good."

"Glad you like it." Mom wiped her hands on a damp cloth. "By the way, Jo has something to show you."

For a moment Jovan couldn't think what she meant. Painting the kitchen had made him forget all about the petsitting job. Then he remembered, and wished he hadn't.

"Go on, Jo," prompted Mom.

Reluctantly Jovan went into the hall. There was the box, still on the table. He picked it up and brought it to his father.

Dad lifted the lid. "It's a garter snake," he said.

"It belongs to Greg Tutt," said Jovan. "He had to go away so he's asked the Petsitters to take care of it."

Dad frowned. "This is only a traveling box. A snake like this should be in a terrarium. That's a sort of fish tank with a heated bulb. It needs to be kept warm."

"Matthew didn't say anything about keeping it warm. He said it wouldn't need to be fed for at least three days and Greg should be back by then."

"It also needs water."

"Matthew didn't mention water either."

"Some in a bowl will do, but it needs to be changed every day." Dad's frown grew deeper. "Greg should have left good instructions."

Greg probably had left good instructions, Jovan thought, but Matthew had been in such a hurry to get away that he hadn't passed them on.

Then he had a brainstorm. "Sam has a fish tank!" he said. "She bought it at a garage sale in case we got asked to take care of some fish, but we never have. I'll take it over to Sam's house."

Dad nodded. "Sounds like a good idea."

"If you hurry you can do it before we have dinner," said Mom.

"Okay!" Jovan picked up the plastic box and hurried out the door.

Sam's father was working in his den when the doorbell rang. He ignored it, hoping that somebody else would answer. When nobody did, he groaned and went to the front door.

Jovan Roy stood on the doorstep, clutching a plastic box with holes in the lid.

"Greg Tutt asked us to take care of this," he said, thrusting the box at Sam's father. "Could you please ask Sam to keep it in her fish tank until Sunday? Thanks." He hurried away down the path.

Sam's father stared down at the plastic box. Then he shrugged and put it on the hall table before going back to work. "If the doorbell rings again I won't answer," he muttered to himself. "Otherwise I'll never get this cartoon finished before Sam comes back from the station with Aunt Cynthia."

Left alone on the table the box sat motionless. But the lid was no longer firmly in place. It had become unfastened while Jovan was carrying it through the streets, and now,

> gradually,
>> *very* gradually,
>>> it began to open.

Chapter 3

Aunt Cynthia

"Where's my suitcase?" Aunt Cynthia demanded. "What has the driver done with my suitcase?"

"It's all right, Aunt," Sam said soothingly. "He put it in the trunk."

"Oh dear, oh dear!" Aunt Cynthia sat back in the taxi, fanning her face with her gloves. "Such a terrible trip. I'd come to see you more often it it weren't such a terrible trip."

Sam kept quiet. She knew how much Dad dreaded his Aunt Cynthia coming to stay, and how glad he was that she didn't come too often. "A nice old bat," was how he described her, "but a terrible fusspot, forever worrying about dust and dirty dishes and unwashed socks. It drives me crazy!"

All the same, he had made a real effort to clean the house in preparation for her arrival. He had even tried to fix the vacuum cleaner, but it still didn't work right, so he and Sam went around on their hands and knees picking up

every bit of fluff they could find. They had swept out the spare room—including under the bed—and washed the breakfast dishes. The house looked cleaner than it had for weeks.

"Dad was sorry he couldn't come to meet you," Sam told Aunt Cynthia, "But he has to finish a cartoon and send it to his editor first thing tomorrow."

Aunt Cynthia signed. "Dear George, I wish he'd chosen an easier way to earn a living. Drawing those tiny little pictures all day must be so bad for his eyesight."

"Being a cartoonist is a very good way to earn a living," said Sam, springing to her father's defense. "At least it means he can work at home."

"I suppose it does." Aunt Cynthia sighed again. "And how about you, Samantha dear? What do you do with yourself all day when your father's working?"

If there was one thing Sam hated it was being called Samantha. "All sorts of things," she said. "For starters, I belong to a club. There's me and Matthew . . ."

"Matthew and I," corrected Aunt Cynthia.

"Matthew and I and Jovan and Matthew's sister Katie. We take care of other people's . . ."

She stopped, remembering that Aunt Cynthia disapproved of animals. Nasty, dirty creatures, she called them, always leaving messes on the floors and pavements and in public parks. The idea of Sam belonging to a *Pet*sitters Club would horrify her.

"Go on," prompted Aunt Cynthia. "You look after other people's . . ."

"Gardens," finished Sam, just as the taxi stopped.

"Do you indeed?" Aunt Cynthia peered through the window at the overgrown wilderness that surrounded Sam's house. "But not, it would appear, your own."

With another sigh, she heaved herself out of the taxi, paid the driver, and insisted he carry her suitcase up the path.

Sam opened the front door and stepped inside. "Dad, we're home!" she called out.

Aunt Cynthia followed her into the hall. She put on the red-framed glasses that hung from a chain around her neck and inspected her surroundings. "I'd forgotten how big this house is," she remarked. "And how inconvenient. Almost impossible to keep clean."

She ran her finger over the hall table and inspected it for dust, but there wasn't any, just a large plastic box with the lid half-open. "Tsk, tsk," muttered Aunt Cynthia, moving it to one side.

Sam stared at it, puzzled. "That's funny," she said. "I'm sure that wasn't there when I left. Somebody must have delivered something."

She peered inside. The box was empty.

"George!" Aunt Cynthia called in a high, demanding voice. "Where are you? I'm here!"

Dad burst out of the den, looking stressed. "Aunt Cynthia! I'm so sorry, but I was working and forgot the time. You know how it is."

Aunt Cynthia allowed him to kiss her cheek, then held him at arm's length.

"You look tired, George, and you're very thin. Samantha looks thin, too. I hope you've both been eating well."

"Oh, we eat very well," he assured her. "Tonight we're having . . . Sam, what are we having?"

"Chicken pot pie," she said. "That's if you remembered to put it in the oven."

He went pale. "I'll go and do it now."

"Dad, wait." She followed him to the kitchen door. "Where did that plastic box come from?"

"Er, somebody brought it." Dad frowned, thinking hard. "I believe it was Jovan Roy. Yes, I'm sure it was Jo. He wants you to take care of it for him."

"But it's empty. Why does he want me to take care of it?"

"I'm not sure. He said something about putting it in a fish tank."

Aunt Cynthia coughed daintily. "Are you going to leave me standing here all night? After that terrible trip I'd like to freshen myself up."

"Yes, of course. Sam, take Aunt Cynthia up to her room." He disappeared into the kitchen.

Reluctantly, Sam picked up Aunt Cynthia's suitcase and started to climb the stairs.

44

Chapter 4

Chicken Pot Pie and Frozen Peas

By the time Aunt Cynthia came downstairs again Sam was busy setting the table for dinner.

"There!" said Aunt Cynthia, seating herself on the sofa. "Now I feel more civilized. What time is dinner?"

"Soon," said Sam. "I'll just go and see how Dad's doing."

She entered the kitchen to find her father frantically searching for dinner plates. "We washed them all," she reminded him. "And put them away."

"So we did. No wonder I can't find anything." He opened a cabinet. "Where's Aunt Cynthia?"

"In the living room, waiting for her dinner."

"It won't be long now." He set three plates on a tray, then clapped a hand to his forehead. "Oh, no! I haven't cooked any vegetables. If we don't give her vegetables she'll say we're not having a healthy diet."

"The chicken pot pie has vegetables," Sam said. "Carrots and loads of potatoes inside."

"Yes, but not *green* vegetables. Do we have any frozen peas?"

"Plenty," said Sam. "I'll boil some water."

She was just taking the bag out of the freezer when Aunt Cynthia came through the door.

"I've come to help," she announced.

"That won't be necessary, Aunt," Dad said quickly. "Everything's under control."

Ignoring him, she opened the oven door and peered inside. "Well, the pie looks all right. Browning nicely on top." She straightened up. "What vegetables are we having?"

"Er, these," said Sam, holding up the bag.

"Frozen peas? Oh well, I suppose they'll have to do." She put on her glasses and looked at the saucepan.

"Water's almost boiling. Give them to me, Samantha." She grabbed them and turned to the stove.

Suddenly she gave a piercing shriek and leaped backwards, dropping the bag. It burst as it hit the floor, scattering small green peas, hard as marbles, in all directions.

Sam and her father stood transfixed, staring at her.

"Oh, oh, oh, oh!" panted Aunt Cynthia. Holding on to the countertop for support, she gazed fixedly at a spot on the kitchen floor. "Oh, whatever was that?"

"Whatever was what, Aunt?" asked Dad.

"That, that *thing* on the floor! I nearly stepped on it."

"I can't see anything," said Sam, staring at the same spot.

"No, well, it's gone now." She pressed a hand to her chest as if to calm her beating heart. "Ugh, I've never seen anything so horrible in my life!"

"What did it look like?" asked Dad.

"Long and thin, like a, a snake." Aunt Cynthia shuddered.

"Probably a piece of string," said Dad. "Or a bit of old plastic."

"It most certainly wasn't! This was alive, I tell you. I distinctly saw it move. I saw it *wriggle*!"

Sam wanted to laugh. She didn't dare look at her father.

"Well, it must have wriggled away," said Dad, "because there's nothing there now."

"Except frozen peas." Sam took the dustpan and broom from the closet and started to clean up the peas.

"Oh, do be careful!" shrieked Aunt Cynthia. "It's probably lying in wait somewhere, waiting to strike."

Dad sighed. "There's nothing there, Aunt, I promise you. It must have been your imagination."

"You should know by now, George, that I don't have any imagination." She turned her back to them. "I will go back into the dining room and wait for my dinner."

A little shakily, but with dignity, she marched out of the kitchen.

Sam giggled. "At least it got rid of her."

"It also got rid of the peas." Dad stared down at the dustpan full of small green marbles. "Unless?"

Sam shook her head. "We can't cook them now. She'd guess."

"In that case, she'll have to have chicken pot pie without vegetables. After all, it's not our fault." He grabbed a potholder and took the pie out of the oven.

"Dad, what do you think she saw?"

"Heaven only knows. I'll carry the pie, you bring the tray."

As they walked through the hall to the dining room, Sam noticed that the plastic box was still on the table and wondered again why Jo brought it over. What did he want her to do with it?

Something about putting it in a fish tank, Dad had said.

But why?

Why should Jo ask her to put an empty box inside a fish tank? It didn't make sense. Mystified, she shook her head and followed her father into the dining room.

"At last!" Aunt Cynthia, now recovered from her fright, had seated herself at the table, waiting for her dinner. "Well, the pie looks very nice anyway, even if there aren't any fresh vegetables. I'll have a large helping, please, George. After all this excitement, I'm feeling quite hungry."

Chapter 5

A Hideous Creature

On Saturday morning, Jovan began to wonder.

He wondered how Sam was getting along with Gertie.

He wondered if she was angry with him for leaving Gertie at her house without first asking if she minded. After all, she might not like snakes any more than he did.

He wondered if he should go over to see her this morning and make sure everything was okay.

In the end, he decided to stop wondering and GO.

To his surprise, a strange woman answered the door. She was short, with a pair of red-framed glasses hanging from a chain around her neck. "Yes?" she said "Did you want something?"

"I came to see Sam," Jovan stammered. "I'm a friend of hers. My name's Jo."

"Wait there," the woman commanded. "I will inform Sam*antha* that you wish to speak to her."

She disappeared. Jovan waited

In a little while, Sam came to the door with a dustrag in her hand. She looked hot and flustered. "Hello, Jo,"

she said. "I'm afraid I can't do any petsitting jobs this weekend. We have Aunt Cynthia staying with us. Didn't Matthew tell you?"

"No, he didn't," said Jo. "Sorry, I wouldn't have left Gertie with you if I'd known."

"Gertie?"

"The, er . . ." Jo was about to say "snake," but then he saw Aunt Cynthia hovering behind Sam and decided against it. Instead he said evasively, "The, . . . er, box."

Sam looked puzzled. "The box is called Gertie?"

"No, not the *box*." Jo lowered his voice. "What was *inside* the box."

"But there wasn't anything inside the box."

"Yes, there was. Didn't you look?"

"Of course I looked. It was empty."

"But . . ."

"Really, Samantha," interrupted Aunt Cynthia. "If you intend to make this a long conversation, I suggest you invite your friend inside. It isn't polite to keep him standing on the doorstep."

"Yes, Aunt Cynthia." Sam opened the door wider.

Jo stepped into the hall. The first thing he saw was the box on the hall table. Then he noticed that the lid was open.

"Where is she?" he demanded. "Have you put her in the fish tank?"

"Where's who?" asked Sam. "Have I put who in the fish tank?"

"Samantha, where are your manners?" said Aunt Cynthia. "Take him into the living room. Offer him a cup of coffee."

Sam looked uncomfortable. "I don't think Jo likes coffee, Aunt."

"Lemonade, then." She turned to Jovan. "I'm sure you'd like *something* to drink, young man?"

Jovan said nervously, "A glass of milk would be nice."

"A glass of milk?" She beamed at him. "Indeed, what could be healthier! I will go and get you one myself!"

She marched towards the kitchen.

"Whew!" said Sam when she was safely out of earshot. "I'm glad you chose milk. She has a thing about healthy eating."

"Actually I hate milk," Jovan confessed. "But I knew I had to choose something. She seems a bit, well forceful."

"Forceful? It's like our house has been hit by a tornado! She made me dust all over this morning, even though I told her I'd already done it before she came. She says she believes in dusting *every day*!" Sam giggled. "Dad's hiding in the den. I think he's scared to come out."

"Did he give you my message?"

"About the box? He said you wanted me to look after it but he didn't say why. I was going to call you as soon as I got the chance."

Jovan stared at her. "You mean you haven't found it?"

"Found what?"

"Greg Tutt's garter sn . . ."

He was interrupted by a piercing shriek from the kitchen.

Sam groaned. "Oh, not again!" She raised her voice. "All right, Aunt. I'm coming."

She dashed into the kitchen.

Jovan followed at a slower pace to find Aunt Cynthia shivering on a chair, her face as white as chalk. A cabinet door stood open and on the floor lay an ever-widening pool of milk.

"I tell you, it *was* there!" she babbled. "I'd just taken a carton of milk from the fridge and, and I went to the cabinet to get a glass and, and that's when I saw it, curled up on the shelf."

"Well, there's nothing there now," said Sam. "Is there, Jo?"

He stared hard at the cabinet, although he wasn't sure what he was supposed to be looking for. "I can't see anything," he admitted.

"No, because it wriggled away again," Aunt Cynthia said defiantly. "And please don't tell me I imagined it. I couldn't possibly dream up such a, a hideous creature!"

"What hideous creature?" Jo asked Sam in a low voice. "What's she talking about?"

"Oh, she keeps thinking she's seen a snake, but of course that's impossible." Sam picked up the empty milk carton. "I'd better clear up this mess before someone steps in it."

Jovan cleared his throat. "Actually, it's not impossible."

"What's going on?" Sam's father

appeared in the doorway. "Don't tell me it's another snake alarm?"

Sam sighed. "I'm afraid so."

"George, you must call the exterminator *at once*," Aunt Cynthia commanded. "This whole house needs to be fumigated."

"Now, Aunt," he said wearily. "I give you my word, there is NO SNAKE IN THIS HOUSE. Not one. So you can safely come down from that chair."

Reluctantly she accepted his outstretched hand. "Very well. But I warn you, if I see it again I will dial 911."

He escorted Aunt Cynthia from the kitchen.

Jovan cleared his throat again. "Er, Sam," he said, "I think there's something you should know."

Chapter 6

Going Crazy

Sam stared at him. "A garter snake?"

Jovan nodded. "Her name's Gertie and she belongs to Greg Tutt."

"And she was definitely in the box when you brought it to me?"

"Oh, yes. I'm sure of it."

For a moment Sam was silent. Then she giggled. "Poor Aunt Cynthia. So she

was right all along, and none of us believed her. No wonder she was so scared."

They both gazed down at the floor, which was still covered with milk.

Sam sighed. "I'd better clean up this mess."

"I'll help you," said Jovan, "And then we can start hunting for Gertie."

They mopped up the milk and washed the kitchen floor until it shone. When they had finished, Sam squeezed the mop and put it outside the back door to dry.

"What I don't understand," she said, "is why Matthew didn't give her to Katie to take care of. She's supposed to be the expert on creepy-crawlies."

"He said she was busy." Jovan opened the door of the china cabinet and peered inside. "Nothing in here."

"It might help if you told me what Gertie looks like," said Sam.

"Well, she's not very big," said Jovan, looking under the sink. "And she's sort of brown with yellow stripes down her back."

"Okay." Sam searched the broom closet. "No snake in here."

"Or in this one."

Sam stood still, thinking. "I wonder why Gertie headed for the kitchen. Do you think she was hunting for food?"

Jovan shook his head. "Matthew said she wouldn't need to be fed for at least three days. Most likely she was looking for someplace warm."

At that moment, Dad came back into the kitchen. "Oh, you've cleaned up," he said. "Good job."

Sam began, "Er, Dad . . ."

"I've managed to calm Aunt Cynthia down, thank goodness." Dad chuckled. "So let's hope that's the last we hear of the phantom snake."

Sam tried again. "Er, Dad . . ."

But this time she was interrupted by a piercing shrink from the living room.

"Oh, no!" Dad groaned. "I don't believe it."

They all raced into the living room to find Aunt Cynthia crouched on a table, clutching her glasses.

"Another one!" she gasped, pointing with a shaking finger. "There by the fireplace."

75

Everyone stared at the fireplace, but there was nothing to be seen.

"Dozens of snakes, all over the house," she moaned. "Hundreds! Thousands! They're following me around."

"Now, Aunt," said Dad in a comforting voice, "I've already given you my word there are no snakes in this house. Do you understand me? NO SNAKES! I think maybe you should see a doctor."

"Are you trying to tell me I'm going crazy?" She glared at him furiously.

"No, of course not. Come, let me help you down."

Reluctantly Aunt Cynthia allowed herself to be coaxed down from the table.

Sam tugged at her father's sleeve. "Dad, can I speak to you, please?"

"What, now?"

"Yes, now! Outside, in the hall. It's important."

"Oh, all right." He followed Sam into the hall. "Okay, what is it?"

Sam said, "Actually, Dad, there is a snake. Her name's Gertie and she came in that box Jo brought over, only the lid was loose and she escaped."

"Escaped?" he repeated faintly. "You mean, Aunt Cynthia isn't going crazy after all?"

Sam shook her head.

At that moment the doorbell rang. Dad groaned. "Oh, no! The last thing we need right now is visitors."

Sam opened the door. Three people stood on the step, Matthew, Katie, and a boy with short red hair.

"This is Greg Tutt," said Matthew. "His grandmother is much better so he came home early, and he wants his snake back."

Chapter 7

Where's Gertie?

"We're busy right now," Sam said. "You'll have to come back later."

She tried to shut the door but Matthew pushed against it.

"It will only take a minute," he said. "Just give him the snake back."

Sam blushed. "I, I can't."

"Why not?" Greg Tutt peered into

the hall. "She must be here. I can see the box."

Quickly Dad blocked Greg's view before he had a chance to notice that the lid was open. "Sorry," he said, "but there's been a slight hitch. My fault, I'm afraid."

"George, what are you doing out there?" Aunt Cynthia appeared in the doorway with Jovan close behind her. "Goodness gracious, more visitors! Samantha, where are your manners? Invite them in."

Sam had no choice but to open the door wider. Matthew, Katie, and Greg trooped into the hall, staring at Aunt Cynthia as if she were a visitor from another planet.

"Well?" she demanded. "Aren't you going to introduce me to your friends?"

"Er, yes," said Sam. "This is Matthew and his sister Katie. And this is Greg Tutt."

"How d'you do," said Aunt Cynthia grandly. "Can we help you in any way?"

"Yes," said Greg Tutt. "You can give me my . . ."

"Box," said Dad. Swiftly closing the lid, he held it out to Greg. "Here you are. Now you can go. Goodbye."

"Really, George!" Aunt Cynthia exclaimed. "You're as bad as Samantha. Come inside, everyone."

Meekly they all trooped into the living room. Matthew and Jovan perched on chairs and Katie sat on the sofa beside Aunt Cynthia. Greg wouldn't sit down, but stood in front of the fireplace, clutching his (empty) plastic box.

Katie smiled up at Aunt Cynthia. "Do you like barnacles?" she inquired.

"Barnacles?" Aunt Cynthia looked puzzled.

"People think they're dull because they don't move much, but if you keep them in water they can get quite lively. And they do have legs, you know."

"Do they indeed?"

Katie nodded. "They use them to kick food up their bottoms. That's how they eat."

"Really?" said Aunt Cynthia faintly. "How fascinating."

At that moment, Sam saw Greg Tutt begin to lift the lid of the box. "*Don't open it!*" she shouted. "*Don't look inside!*"

Now it was Greg's turn to look puzzled. "I just wanted to see if Gertie was okay."

"She's okay. She's fine." Sam glowered at him. "Take my word for it."

Greg stared at her, the lid half open.

Dad cleared his throat. "Sam and Matthew and Jovan and Katie all belong to a club, Aunt."

"Ah, yes," said Aunt Cynthia, nodding. "Samantha told me. You look after people's gardens, I believe?"

This time everyone looked puzzled.

Then Sam saw it.

She saw it quite clearly.

A slender brown snake

with yellow markings

under Aunt Cynthia's chair was

wriggling,

wriggling,

wriggling,

closer and closer to Aunt Cynthia's foot,

winding itself around the heel of

Aunt Cynthia's shoe.

"I *said*," Aunt Cynthia repeated, rather testily, "you take care of people's garden, I believe?"

No one answered. By now everyone had seen the snake and was watching, fascinated, to see if it would start climbing up Aunt Cynthia's ankle.

"Is something wrong?" she asked.

"Gertie!" gasped Greg Tutt, pointing. "That's Gertie!"

Aunt Cynthia looked alarmed. "What?"

Sam leaped forward. "Dirty!" she said. "On the carpet. A dirty mark. Lift up your foot, Aunt. I'll clean it off."

She knelt down and lifted Aunt Cynthia's shoe, dislodging Gertie who fell to the floor and started to wriggle

away. But Matthew moved equally quickly. He grabbed Gertie and shoved her into the half-opened box.

"Quick, close the lid," he hissed at Greg. Startled, Greg obeyed.

Aunt Cynthia stared down at the carpet. "I don't see any dirty mark," she said.

"No, it's gone now. Just a piece of old twig," said Sam. "I bet someone brought it in from the garden on their shoe."

Matthew moved to the door. "We have to go," he said. "Come on, everyone."

"Bye, kids," said Dad, grinning broadly. "Nice to see you."

Sam followed them into the hall. "Don't forget to ask Greg to sign the form," she muttered to Matthew. "Otherwise we won't get any points."

"You must be joking!" said Matthew. "Between us we nearly lost his snake."

"Yes, but we didn't, did we? He got her back safely."

Sam shut the door behind them and returned to the living room.

Her father still had a grin on his face. "I've just been saying to Aunt Cynthia, I bet that's what she saw. A twig from the garden must have stuck to her shoe, and that's why she thought it was following her around."

Aunt Cynthia looked doubtful. "I suppose you could be right."

"I'm sure I am. You can be quite certain, Aunt, there is *no snake* anywhere in this house!" He winked at Sam.

"Oh dear, all this excitement has made me tired. I think I'll go upstairs and have a little nap." Aunt Cynthia struggled to her feet. When she reached the door she stopped and said, "I must say, though, it was a very *wriggly* sort of twig."

Sam and her father only just managed to keep their faces straight until the door had closed safely behind her.

On Sunday, after Aunt Cynthia had gone home, Sam found her father chuckling at his drawing board.

"It's fine for you to laugh," she grumbled. "Matthew just called to tell me that Greg Tutt refused to sign our community service form. He said we hadn't taken care of Gertie well and we obviously weren't experts on snakes. That's the Petsitters' first failure."

"Oh, I wouldn't say that," said Dad. "It's given me a great idea for a story."

Sam looked over his shoulder and saw that he had drawn a series of cartoons featuring a short lady with red-framed glasses. In each picture the short lady was doing something different—reading a book, cutting roses, washing the dishes—not realizing there was a snake half-hidden in the background.

"I thought I'd call it 'Where's Gertie?'"
he told Sam. "Could make my fortune."
  Sam giggled. "Poor Aunt Cynthia. If
only she'd known!"

The End

The Petsitters Club

JOIN NOW!

You will receive:

- A membership certificate imprinted with your name!
- The official Petsitters Club newsletter sent to you four times a year
- A special "Members Only" Petsitters Club poster
- A Petsitters Club stuffed animal

Mail this coupon today to:

Barron's Educational Series, Inc., Dept. PC
250 Wireless Blvd., Hauppauge, NY 11788 • www.barronseduc.com

---

YES! I want to become a member of The Petsitters Club!

Please send my membership kit to:

Name _____

Address _____

City _____

State _____ Zip _____

Phone ( ) _____ Age _____

BARRON'S

Offer good in U.S. and Canada only.

Join The Petsitters Club for *more* animal adventures!